Once Upon a Cloud

written by

ROB D. WALKER

illustrated by

MATT MAHURIN

THE BLUE SKY PRESS
An Imprint of Scholastic Inc. • New York

for Grandma,
Momma, my wife,
and my children
R. D. W.

THE BLUE SKY PRESS

MAY 0 2 2005

Text copyright © 2005 by Rob D. Walker   Illustrations copyright © 2005 by Matt Mahurin   All rights reserved.
No part of this publication may be reproduced, or stored in a retrieval system, or transmitted in any form or by any means, electronic, mechanical,
photocopying, recording, or otherwise, without written permission of the publisher.   For information regarding permission, please write to:
Permissions Department, Scholastic Inc., 557 Broadway, New York, New York 10012.   SCHOLASTIC, THE BLUE SKY PRESS, and associated logos
are trademarks and/or registered trademarks of Scholastic Inc.   Library of Congress catalog card number: 2004007856   ISBN 0-439-68879-5
10 9 8 7 6 5 4 3 2 1   05 06 07 08 09   Printed in Singapore   46   First printing, February 2005

for Fiona
and James
M. M.

What are clouds made of?

And why do they float?

Are skies the water

and clouds the boat?

So many sizes

and so many shapes!

No two are alike—

just like snowflakes. . . .

Like huge balls of cotton,

they drift through the sky

so you almost can touch them. . . .

Just reach way up high!

Maybe clouds are made

by a special machine

in a cloud-making factory

we've never seen.

Or are clouds the exhaust

from alien ships

that leave puffy trails

when they go on their trips?

Are clouds drifting cities,
and then when it squalls,
the people splash down
in each raindrop that falls?

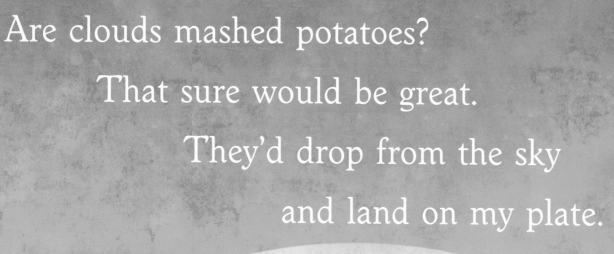

Are clouds mashed potatoes?
That sure would be great.
They'd drop from the sky
and land on my plate.

Are clouds whirling wind

in a swirl-away rush?

I hope they'll slow down

for my paper and brush!

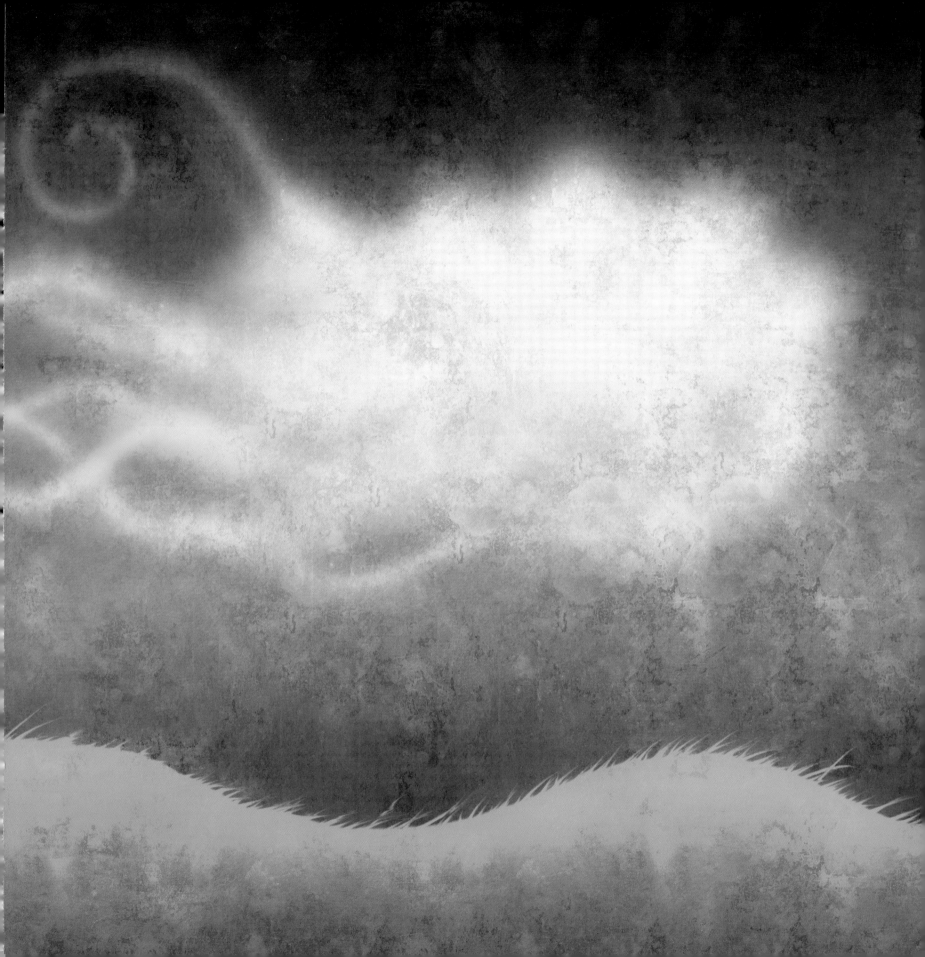

Are clouds cotton candy

for giants to eat?

Do they fly fast as jets?

Are they sticky and sweet?

No, clouds must be ice cream—

a cool, tasty treat,

a scoop of vanilla

for angels to eat.

Are clouds puffs of smoke
from Grandfather's pipe—

or a monster that swallows
your runaway kite?

Are clouds comfy cushions

where birds take their naps,

resting their wings

and hiding from cats?

I just thought of something—

maybe it's weird . . .

but what if the clouds
are Father Time's beard?

I know what they are.

I've figured it out.

Clouds are just dreams . . .

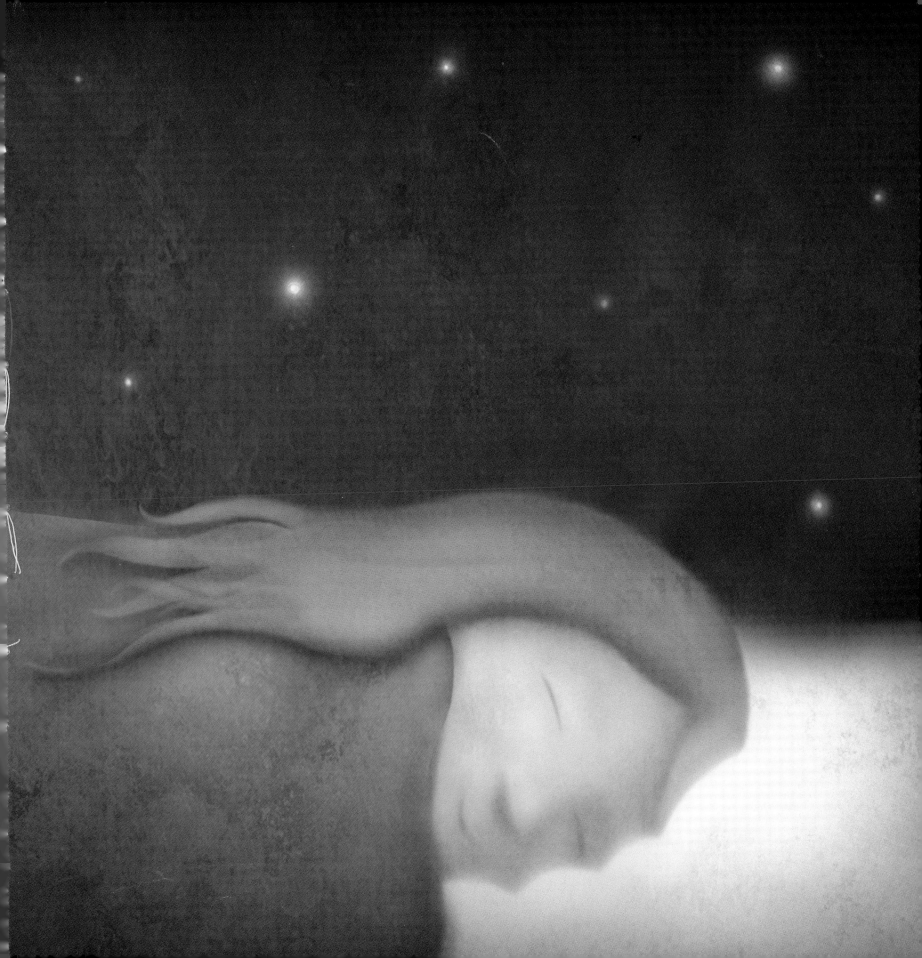

. . . that wander about.

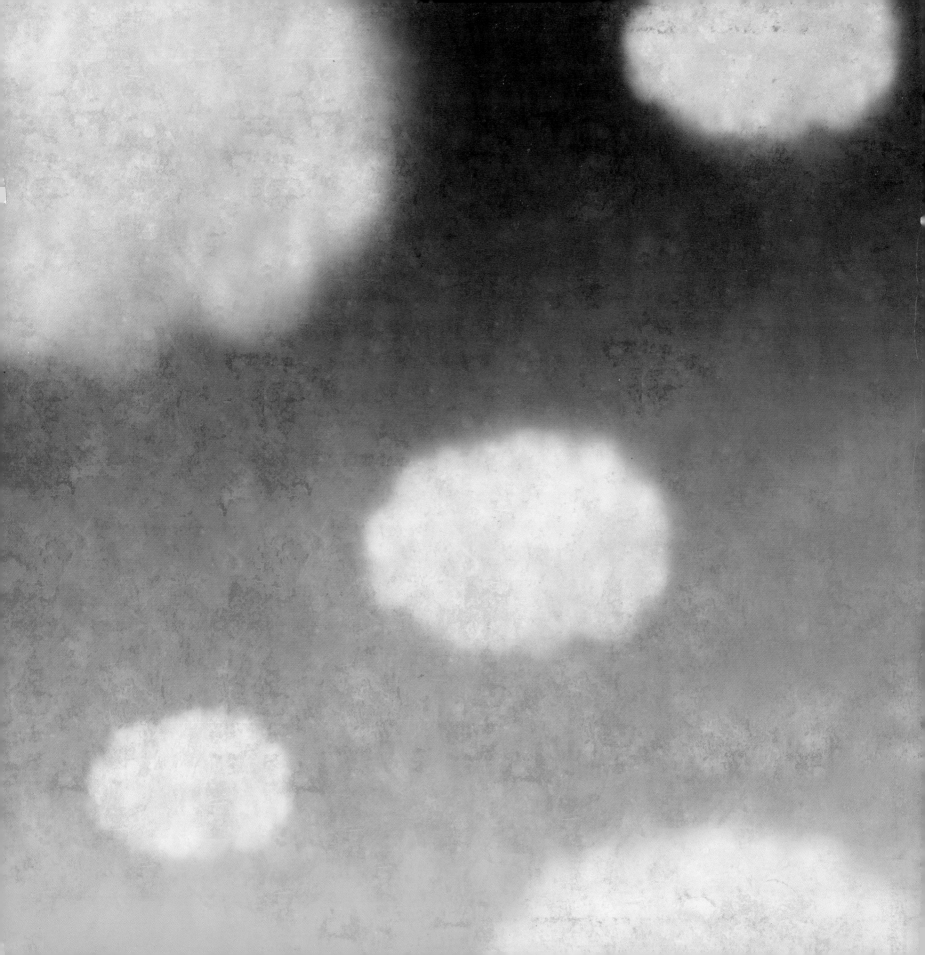